BIG MAX

KIN PLATT

illustrated by
ROBERT LOPSHIRE

HarperCollins*Publishers*

*To the memory of
Charles F. Mintz,
a great detective*

HarperCollins®, ﷼®, and I Can Read Book®
are trademarks of HarperCollins Publishers Inc.

Big Max
Text copyright © 1965 by Kin Platt
Illustrations copyright © 1965, 1992 by Robert Lopshire
Manufactured in China. All rights reserved.

For information address HarperCollins Children's
Books, a division of HarperCollins Publishers,
10 East 53rd Street, New York, NY 10022.
www.harpercollinschildrens.com
Newly Illustrated Edition

Library of Congress Cataloging-in-Publication Data
Platt, Kin.
  Big Max / by Kin Platt ; illustrations by Robert Lopshire.
    p.   cm.— (An I can read book)
  Summary: Big Max, the world's greatest detective, helps a king
find his missing elephant.
  ISBN 0-06-024750-9. — ISBN 0-06-024751-7 (lib. bdg.)
  ISBN 0-06-444006-0 (pbk.)
  [1. Mystery and detective stories.   2. Elephants—Fiction.]
I. Lopshire, Robert, ill.   II. Title.   III. Series.
PZ7.P7125Bi   1992   91-14742
[E]—dc20   CIP
                                                            AC

11 12 13 SCP 20 19 18 17 16 15

BIG MAX

Big Max was the world's

greatest detective.

Everyone knew it.

The King of Pooka Pooka knew it.

He called Big Max on the telephone.

"Come quickly," he cried.
"Someone has stolen Jumbo,
my prize elephant."

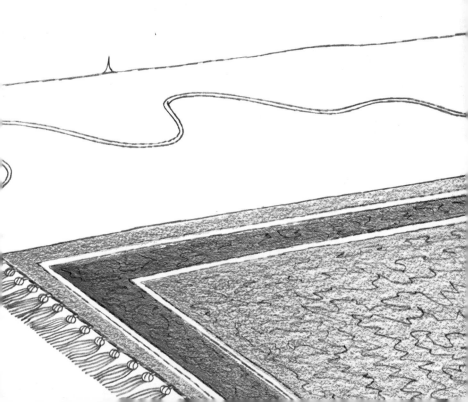

"Do not worry," said Big Max.

"I will be right there.

I will find him for you."

"Will you come by plane or boat?"
the King asked.

"By umbrella," Big Max said.

Big Max took a deep breath.

He blew into his umbrella.

The umbrella filled with air.

Big Max flew through the sky.

On the way he met some birds.

"We are flying south for the winter,"

said the birds. "What are you doing?"

"I am looking for a missing elephant,"

Big Max said.

"You won't find him up here,"

said one of the birds.

"But feel free to look around."

"Thank you," said Big Max.

They flew over a ship.

"I smell something burning,"

said Big Max.

"Sorry we can't help you.

Birds can't smell," said the birds.

Big Max flew down to the ship.

He spoke to the Captain.

"Pardon me," Big Max said.

"I smell something burning."

The Captain laughed.

"Ha, ha," he said.

"That is the smoke

from the smokestacks."

"This smoke

is coming from your pocket,"

Big Max said.

18

"My pipe!" cried the Captain.

He took it out of his pocket.

"I forgot it was still lit.

You are a great detective."

"I try to be," said Big Max.

Big Max flew on.

It began to rain.

"It's a good thing I travel

by umbrella," Big Max said.

When he came to Pooka Pooka,

Big Max flew down.

The King was waiting for him.

"That is a great way to travel,"

the King said.

"It got me here," said Big Max.

The King led Big Max to the palace.

"I will give you anything I have

if you will find Jumbo," he said.

"I will find him," said Big Max.

The King showed Big Max

a room full of rubies.

He showed him

a room full of emeralds.

He showed him

a room full of gold.

"Do you charge a lot?"

asked the King.

"Not that much," said Big Max.

"Who would want to steal Jumbo?"
asked Big Max.

"Everybody," said the King,

"because Jumbo is the

best elephant in the world."

"How old is Jumbo?" Big Max asked.

"He will be four years old tomorrow,"
said the King.

"Ah!" said Big Max.

"Is that a clue?" asked the King.

"We shall see," said Big Max.

"Was Jumbo happy here?"
asked Big Max.

"He was very happy," said the King.

"Until a week ago."

"What happened then?"

asked Big Max.

"He became sad," said the King.

"It is the first time he has been sad

since I got him,"

the King said.

"When did you get him?"

asked Big Max.

"Almost a year ago," said the King.

"Take me to where

you last saw Jumbo," said Big Max.

The King led him outside.

He opened a lock on the gate.

"Here," he said.

"In this courtyard."

27

Big Max looked all around.

He looked up at the high walls.

"Elephants cannot climb walls,"

said Big Max.

Big Max looked at the gate.

"Was the gate locked?" he asked.

"Yes," said the King.

"And I have the only key."

"Hmm," Big Max said.

"Elephants cannot open locks."

Big Max looked at the ground.

"Jumbo was not stolen!" he said.

"How do you know?" asked the King.

"There are no footprints

except Jumbo's," said Big Max.

"Then how did he get out?"

asked the King.

"We shall see," said Big Max.

"I see a clue," said Big Max.

"The ground is wet. Did it rain?"

"It always rains in Pooka Pooka,"

said the King.

"Perhaps you are not

such a great detective after all."

"We shall see," said Big Max.

31

It was very hot.

Big Max sat down to think.

"What a wonderful idea," he said.

"An ice chair for hot days."

"Jumbo likes to sit on ice too,"

said the King.

"That is why I always have

so much ice here."

"I do not see much ice," said Big Max.

"Only little pieces."

Big Max looked down.

He was sitting on the ground.

"This ice melts very fast,"

Big Max said.

"What is on the other side
of the wall?" he asked.

"A high hill," said the King.

"Ha!" said Big Max.

"Now I know how Jumbo did it.

We must look outside the wall,"

Big Max said. "Hurry!"

They hurried outside the wall.

They hurried down the hill.

"Ha!" said Big Max. "I was right.

Look. Here are tracks."

"You are right," said the King.

"These could be Jumbo's tracks,"

said Big Max.

"We must follow them."

They followed the tracks.

"If we find out where Jumbo went,"
said Big Max, "we may find out
why he went."

"I see," said the King.

"Ha!" said Big Max.

"I see another clue. I see tears."

The King looked at the clue.

"I do not know why

Jumbo was so unhappy," he said.

"We shall see," said Big Max.

"If we know *why* Jumbo went,"
said Big Max, "then we will know
where he went."

"I see," said the King.

"You are a great detective."

"Look and think," said Big Max.

"That is the secret."

They followed the trail of the tracks.

They followed the trail of the tears.

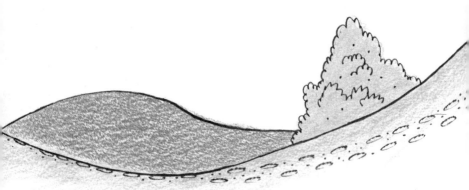

They walked all night.

They walked all the next day.

The trail went uphill.

They followed it.

Suddenly Big Max stopped.

"Wait," Big Max said.

"Something is wrong.

We are following the wrong trail.

Hurry!"

They went down the hill.

They hurried.

Then they heard a loud sound.

"AAAAAAARGH!"

"What was that?" asked the King.

"Well," said Big Max. "Let us think.

It was not an elephant.

Elephants do not sound like that.

They do not say AAAAAAARGH!"

Big Max said, "Just as I thought.

These are not elephant tears.

These are crocodile tears.

They are bigger

than elephant tears."

"Let us think," said Big Max.

"This path has long sharp white teeth.

It has a long red tongue.

It has crocodile tears

instead of elephant tears.

So it must be a crocodile."

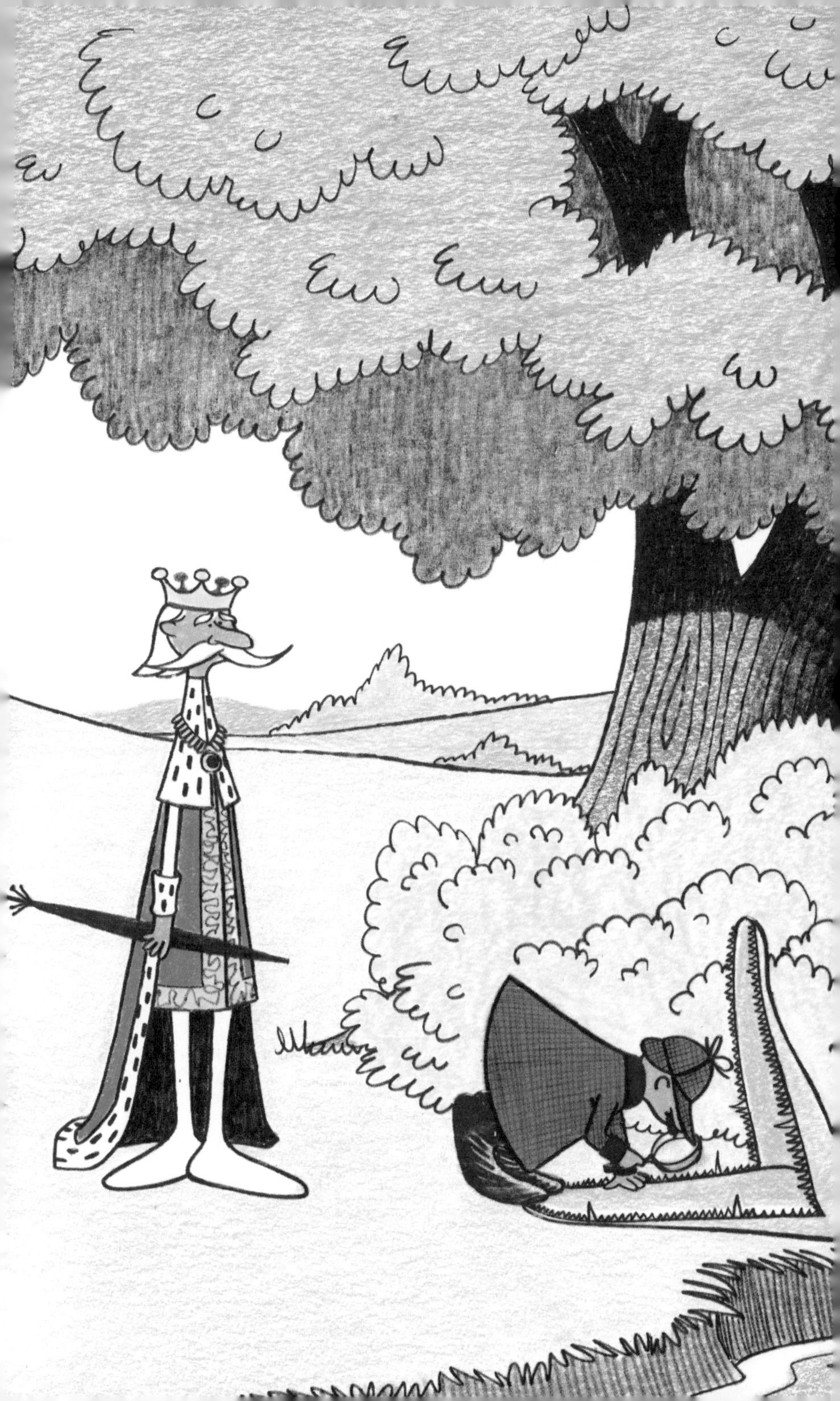

Big Max turned around.

"I was right. It is a crocodile,"

said Big Max. "See for yourself."

"I take your word for it,"

said the King.

"It is a good thing

I came by umbrella," Big Max said.

"He cannot bite now."

Big Max pushed the crocodile

into the water.

Then he took out his umbrella.

"You nearly fooled me

with that wrong clue,"

he said to the crocodile.

"I'm so sorry," the crocodile said.

A big tear rolled out of his eye.

"Look, he is crying," said the King.

"That means he is sorry."

"A crocodile's tears can fool you,"

said Big Max.

"He is crying because he did not

have us for dinner."

"Don't remind me," said the crocodile.

He cried some more.

Big Max and the King

went back to the right trail.

They walked through the jungle.

They heard a lot of noise.

The noise got louder.

The ground shook.

The trees shook. Big Max

and the King of Pooka Pooka shook.

"We must turn back," said the King.

"It is an earthquake."

"No," said Big Max.

"It is not an earthquake.

It is a party."

"A party?" asked the King.

"An elephant party," said Big Max.

He pointed through the trees.

"Look," Big Max said.

There were a lot of elephants.

They were dancing.

They danced so hard

the ground shook.

"There is Jumbo," said the King.

"I see him. He is dancing too."

Big Max smiled.

"Another case solved," he said.

"It is a birthday party for Jumbo,"
said Big Max.

"That is why he went away.

To spend his birthday

with his family."

The King ran to Jumbo.

"Happy birthday, Jumbo," he said.

"How did you find me?" asked Jumbo.

"Ask Big Max," said the King.

"We followed your trail
to find out *where* you went
and to find out *why* you went,"
said Big Max.
"I would still like to know
how he went," said the King.

"It was the ice," said Big Max.

"Jumbo took the cakes of ice.

He put one on top of another.

He made steps out of them.

He fooled me at first,

because there were no steps to see.

Only some melting ice."

"Jumbo walked up the steps of ice.

He walked to the top of the wall.

Behind the wall was a high hill.

He walked over the wall.

He walked down the hill."

"Yes," said Jumbo. "That is how."

"Now I know *how* you went.

Now I know *where* you went.

Now I know *why* you went,"

the King said.

"I did not know a birthday party

was so important."

"It is for elephants," said Big Max.

"Elephants like to be together.

Especially on birthdays."

"I am sorry I did not know,"

said the King of Pooka Pooka.

"Next year I will invite

all your family

to a birthday party at the palace.

That way we can all be together."

"You are a very great detective,"

the King said to Big Max.

"You can have any of my treasures

as a reward for finding Jumbo."

"If you don't mind," said Big Max,

"I would rather have

a piece of Jumbo's birthday cake."

"I don't mind," said the King.

Jumbo gave Big Max and the King
pieces of cake.

"My, what good cake,"
the King said.

Then he ate another piece.

And then one more.

"Don't eat too much," said Jumbo.

"Or I won't be able to carry you
back to Pooka Pooka."

The King stopped eating cake.

"Happy birthday, Jumbo," he said.

"Happy birthday, Jumbo,"
said Jumbo's family.

"Happy birthday, Jumbo,"

said Big Max.

He took a deep breath.

He blew into his umbrella.

"And good-bye," said Big Max,

the greatest detective in the world.